CHILDREN'S THRIFT CLASSICS

Favorite
North American
Indian Legends

EDITED BY PHILIP SMITH

Illustrated by Thea Kliros

DOVER PUBLICATIONS, INC.
New York

DOVER CHILDREN'S THRIFT CLASSICS

Copyright

Copyright © 1994 by Dover Publications, Inc.

All rights reserved under Pan American and International Copyright Conventions.

Published in Canada by General Publishing Company, Ltd., 30 Lesmill Road, Don Mills, Toronto, Ontario.

Published in the United Kingdom by Constable and Company, Ltd., 3 The Lanchesters, 162–164 Fulham Palace Road, London W6 9ER.

Bibliographical Note

This Dover edition, first published in 1994, is a new anthology containing the unabridged text of thirteen works selected from the following: Charles G. Leland, *The Algonquin Legends of New England; or, Myths and Folk Lore of the Micmac, Passamaquoddy, and Penobscot Tribes* (Boston: Houghton, Mifflin and Company, 1884; "How Glooskap Conquered the Great Bull-Frog," "How the Toad and the Porcupine Lost Their Noses," "How Master Lox as a Raccoon Killed the Bear and the Black Cats"); Charles F. Lummis, *The Man Who Married the Moon and Other Pueblo Indian Folk-Stories* (New York: The Century Co., 1891; "The Man Who Married the Moon," "The Ants That Pushed on the Sky"); Franz Boas, "Tsimshian Mythology," *Thirty-First Annual Report of the Bureau of American Ethnology to the Secretary of the Smithsonian Institution, 1909–1910* (Washington: Government Printing Office, 1916; "The Story of Grizzly Bear and Beaver," "The Meeting of the Wild Animals"); James Mooney, "Myths of the Cherokee," *Nineteenth Annual Report of the Bureau of American Ethnology to the Secretary of the Smithsonian Institution, 1897–98*, Part 1 (Washington: Government Printing Office, 1900 [1902]; "The Daughter of the Sun," "The Bear Man"); Erminnie A. Smith, "Myths of the Iroquois," *Second Annual Report of the Bureau of Ethnology to the Secretary of the Smithsonian Institution, 1880–'81* (Washington: Government Printing Office, 1883; "The Friendly Skeleton"); Charles A. Eastman and Elaine Goodale Eastman, *Wigwam Evenings: Sioux Folk Tales Retold* (Boston: Little Brown and Company, 1909; "The Laugh-maker," "The Girl Who Married the Star," "The Little Boy Man"). The illustrations and introductory Note have been prepared specially for this edition.

Library of Congress Cataloging-in-Publication-Data

Favorite North American Indian legends / edited by Philip Smith ; illustrated by Thea Kliros.

    p.   cm. — (Dover children's thrift classics)

    ISBN 0-486-27822-0

    1. Indians of North America—Folklore. 2. Legends—United States. I. Smith, Philip, 1967–   II. Kliros, Thea. III. Series.

E98.F6F38 1994

398.2'08997—dc20   94-15680

                                         CIP
                                         AC

Manufactured in the United States of America
Dover Publications, Inc., 31 East 2nd Street, Mineola, N.Y. 11501

Note

The thirteen legends in this collection represent a sampling of stories handed down through generations of various indigenous peoples of North America: the Tsimshian Indians of the Pacific Northwest; the Passamaquoddy of Maine and the Micmac of New Brunswick; the Pueblo of the American Southwest; the Cherokee, the Iroquois and the Sioux.

Like much folklore, many of these legends explain natural phenomena—how the toad and the porcupine lost their noses, or why the loon cries and the wolf howls. There are transformation myths as well, which feature beings such as Glooskap, a powerful divinity who can change shape at will, and Master Lox, who, in his various disguises, creates all manner of mischief for animals and men. And then there are the legends of the strange and wonderful, such as "The Friendly Skeleton" or "The Daughter of the Sun," stories that take us to enchanted islands where the dead come to life, or to the Ghost country in the Darkening land.

Here, then, is an opportunity for children to learn about North America's original cultures through the legends and stories that reflect a unique cultural heritage.

Contents

List of Illustrations

How Glooskap Conquered
the Great Bull-Frog

(PASSAMAQUODDY AND MICMAC)

N'KARNAYOO, of old times, there was an Indian village far away among the mountains, little known to other men. And the dwellers therein were very comfortable: the men hunted every day, the women did the work at home, and all went well in all things save in this. The town was by a brook, and except in it there was not a drop of water in all the country round, unless in a few rain-puddles. No one there had ever found even a spring.

Now these Indians were very fond of good water. The brook was of a superior quality, and they became dainty over it.

But after a time they began to observe that the brook was beginning to run low, and that not in the summer time, but in autumn, even after the rains. And day by day it diminished, until its bed was as dry as a dead bone in the ashes of a warm fire.

Now it was said that far away up in the land where none had ever been there was on this

1

very stream another Indian village; but what manner of men dwelt therein no one knew. And thinking that these people of the upper country might be in some way concerned in the drought, they sent one of their number to go and see into the matter.

And after he had traveled three days he came to the place; and there he found that a dam had been raised across the rivulet, so that no water could pass, for it was all kept in a pond. Then asking them why they had made this mischief, since the dam was of no use to them, they bade him go and see their chief, by whose order this had been built.

And when he came to him, there lay lazily in the mud a creature who was more of a monster than a man, though he had a human form. For he was immense to measure, like a giant, fat, bloated, and brutal to behold. His great yellow eyes stuck from his head like pine-knots, his mouth went almost from ear to ear, and he had broad, skinny feet with long toes, exceeding marvelous.

The messenger complained to this monster, who at first said nothing, and then croaked, and finally replied in a loud bellow,—

"Do as you choose,
Do as you choose,
Do as you choose.

"What do I care?
What do I care?
What do I care?

"If you want water,
If you want water,
If you want water,
Go somewhere else."

Then the messenger remonstrated, and described the suffering of the people, who were dying of thirst. And this seemed to please the monster, who grinned. At last he got up, and, making a single spring to the dam, took an arrow and bored a hole in it, so that a little water trickled out, and then he bellowed,—

"Up and begone!
Up and begone!
Up and begone!"

So the man departed, little comforted. He came to his home, and for a few days there was a little water in the stream; but this soon stopped, and there was great suffering again.

Now these Indians, who were the honestest fellows in all the world, and never did harm to any one save their enemies, were in a sorry pickle. For it is a bad thing to have nothing but water to drink, but to want that is to be mightily dry. And the great Glooskap, who knew all that was passing in the hearts of men and beasts, took note of this, and when he willed it he was among them; for he ever came as the wind comes, and no man wist how.

And just before he came all of these good fellows had resolved in council that they would send the boldest man among them to certain death, even to the village which built the dam that kept the water which filled the brook that quenched their thirst, whenever it was not empty. And when there he was either to obtain that they should cut the dam, or do something desperate, and to this intent he should go armed, and sing his death-song as he went. And they were all agog.

Then Glooskap, who was much pleased with all this, for he loved a brave man, came among them looking terribly ferocious; in all the land there was not one who seemed half so horrible. For he appeared ten feet high, with a hundred red and black feathers in his scalp-lock, his face painted like fresh blood with green rings round his eyes, a large clam-shell hanging from each ear, a spread eagle, very awful to behold, flapping its wings from the back of his neck, so that as he strode into the village all hearts quaked. Being but simple people, they accounted that this must be, if not Lox the Great Wolverine, at least Mitche-hant, the devil himself in person, turned Wabanaki; and they admired him greatly, and the squaws said they had never seen aught so lovely.

Then Glooskap, having heard the whole story, bade them be of good cheer, declaring that he would soon set all to rights. And he without delay departed up the bed of the brook; and coming to the town, sat down and bade a boy bring him water to drink. To which the boy replied that no water could be had in that town unless it were given out by the chief. "Go then to your chief," said the Master, "and bid him hurry, or, verily, I will know the reason why." And this being told, Glooskap received no reply for more than an hour, during which time he sat on a log and smoked his pipe. Then the boy returned with a small cup, and this not half full, of very dirty water.

So he arose, and said to the boy, "I will go and see your chief, and I think he will soon give me better water than this." And having come to the monster, he said, "Give me to drink, and that of the best, at once, thou Thing of Mud!" But the chief reviled him, and said, "Get thee hence, to find water where thou canst." Then Glooskap thrust a spear into his belly, and lo! there gushed forth a mighty

"Give me to drink, and that of the best, at once,
thou Thing of Mud!"

river; even all the water which should have run on while in the rivulet, for he had made it into himself. And Glooskap, rising high as a giant pine, caught the chief in his hand and crumpled in his back with a mighty grip. And lo! it was the Bull-Frog. So he hurled him with contempt into the stream, to follow the current.

And ever since that time the Bull-Frog's back has crumpled wrinkles in the lower part, showing the prints of Glooskap's awful squeeze.

Then he returned to the village; but there he found no people,—no, not one. For a marvelous thing had come to pass during his absence, which shall be heard in every Indian's speech through all the ages. For the men, being, as I said, simple, honest folk, did as boys do when they are hungry, and say unto one another, "What would *you* like to have, and what you?" "Truly, I would be pleased with a slice of hot venison dipped in maple-sugar and bear's oil." "Nay, give me for my share succotash and honey." Even so these villagers had said, "Suppose *you* had all the nice cold, fresh, sparkling, delicious water there is in the world, what would *you* do?"

And one said that he would live in the soft mud, and always be wet and cool.

And another, that he would plunge from the rocks, and take headers, diving into the deep, cold water, drinking as he dived.

And the third, that he would be washed up and down with the rippling waves, living on the land, yet ever in the water.

Then the fourth said, "Verily, you know not how to wish, and I will teach you. I would live in the water all the time, and swim about in it forever."

Now it chanced that these things were said in the hour which, when it passes over the world, all the wishes uttered by men are granted. And so it was with these Indians. For the first became a Leech, the second a Spotted Frog, the third a Crab, which is washed up and down with the tide, and the fourth a Fish. Ere this there had been in all the world none of the creatures which dwell in the water, and now they were there, and of all kinds. And the river came rushing and roaring on, and they all went headlong down to the sea, to be washed into many lands over all the world.

How the Toad and Porcupine
Lost their Noses

(MICMAC)

IN THE old time. Far before men knew
themselves, in the light before the sun,
Glooskap and his brother were as yet unborn;
they waited for the day to appear. Then they
talked together, and the youngest said, "Why
should I wait? I will go into the world and
begin my life at once." Then the elder said,
"Not so, for this were a great evil." But the
younger gave no heed to any wisdom: in his
wickedness he broke through his mother's
side, he rent the wall; his beginning of life was
his mother's death.

Now, in after years, the younger brother
would learn in what lay the secret of the
elder's death. And Glooskap, being crafty, told
the truth and yet lied; for his name was the
Liar, yet did he never lie for evil or aught to
harm. So he told his brother that the blow of a
ball, or handful of the down of feathers,
would take away his life; and this was true,
for it would stun him, but it would not pre-

vent his returning to life. Then Glooskap asked the younger for his own secret. And he, being determined to give the elder no time, answered truly and fearlessly, "I can only be slain by the stroke of a cat-tail or bulrush."

And then the younger, having gathered the down of bird's feathers, struck the elder, so that he fell dead, and therein he told the truth. But he soon recovered, and in that was his deceit. Howbeit it was well for the world and well for him that he then gathered bulrushes and smote his younger brother, so that he died. But the plant never grew that could harm the Master, wherefore he is alive to this day.

Who was his mother? The female Turtle was his mother.

The Master was the Lord of Men and Beasts. Beasts and Men, one as the other, he ruled them all. Great was his army, his tribe was All. In it the Great Golden Eagle was a chief; he married a female Caribou. The Turtle was Glooskap's uncle; he married a daughter of the Golden Eagle and Caribou. Of all these things there are many and long traditions. Our people tell them in the winter by the fire: the old people know them; the young forget them and the wisdom which is in them.

When the Turtle married, the Master bade him make a feast, and wished that the banquet should be a mighty one. To do this he gave him great power. He bade him go down to a point of rocks by the sea, where many whales were always to be found. He bade him bring one; he gave him power to do so, but he set a mark, or an appointed space, and bade him not go an inch beyond it. So the Turtle went down to the sea; he caught a great whale, he bore it to camp; it seemed to him easy to do this. But like all men there was in him vain curiosity; the falsehood of disobedience was in him, and to try the Master he went beyond the mark; and as he did this he lost his magic strength; he became as a man; even as a common mortal his nerves weakened, and he fell, crushed flat beneath the weight of the great fish.

Then men ran to Glooskap, saying that Turtle was dead. But the Master answered, "Cut up the Whale; he who is now dead will revive." So they cut it up; (and when the feast was ready) Turtle came in yawning, and stretching out his leg he cried, "How tired I am! Truly, I must have overslept myself." Now from this time all men greatly feared Glooskap, for they saw that he was a spirit.

It came to pass that the Turtle waxed mighty in his own conceit, and thought that he could take Glooskap's place and reign in his stead. So he held a council of all the animals to find out how he could be slain. The Lord of Men and Beasts laughed at this. Little did he care for them!

And knowing all that was in their hearts, he put on the shape of an old squaw and went into the council-house. And he sat down by two witches: one was the Porcupine, the other the Toad; as women they sat there. Of them the Master asked humbly how they expected to kill him. And the Toad answered savagely, "What is that to thee, and what hast thou to do with this thing?" "Truly," he replied, "I meant no harm," and saying this he softly touched the tips of their noses, and rising went his way. But the two witches, looking one at the other, saw presently that their noses were both gone, and they screamed aloud in terror, but their faces were none the less flat. And so it came that the Toad and the Porcupine both lost their noses and have none to this day.

Glooskap had two dogs. One was the Loon (Kwemoo), the other the Wolf (Malsum). Of old all animals were as men; the Master gave them the shapes which they now bear. But the Wolf and the Loon loved Glooskap so greatly that since he left them they howl and wail. He who hears their cries over the still sound and lonely lake, by the streams where no dwellers are, or afar at night in the forests and hollows, hears them sorrowing for the Master.

The Meeting of the Wild Animals

(TSIMSHIAN)

A LONG TIME ago, when the Tsimshian lived on the upper Skeena River, in Prairie Town, there were many people. They were the most clever and the strongest among all the people, and they were good hunters, and caught many animals, going hunting the whole year round. Therefore all the animals were in great distress on account of the hunters.

Therefore the animals held a meeting. The Grizzly Bear invited all the large animals to his house, and said to them, "We are distressed, and a calamity has befallen us on account of the hunting of these people, who pursue us into our dens. Therefore it is in my mind to ask Him Who Made Us to give us more cold in winter, so that no hunter may come and kill us in our dens. Let Him Who Made Us give to our earth severe cold!" Thus spoke the Grizzly Bear to his guests. Then all the large animals agreed to what the chief had said, and the Wolf spoke: "I have something to say. Let us invite all the small animals,—even

14

such as Porcupine, Beaver, Raccoon, Marten, Mink, down to the small animals such as the Mouse, and the Insects that move on the earth,—for they might come forth and protest against us, and our advice might come to nought!" Thus spoke the large Wolf to the large animals in their council.

Therefore on the following day the large animals assembled on an extensive prairie, and they called all the small animals, down to the insects; and all the small animals and the insects assembled and sat down on one side of the plain, and the large animals were sitting on the other side of the plain. Panther came, Grizzly Bear, Black Bear, Wolf, Elk, Reindeer, Wolverene—all kinds of large animals.

Then the chief speaker, Grizzly Bear, arose, and said, "Friends, I will tell you about my experiences." Thus he spoke to the small animals and to the insects. "You know very well how we are afflicted by the people who hunt us on mountains and hills, even pursuing us into our dens. Therefore, my brothers, we have assembled (he meant the large animals). On the previous day I called them all, and I told them what I had in my mind. I said, 'Let us ask Him Who Made Us to give to our earth cold winters, colder than ever, so that the people who hunt us can not come to our dens

All the small animals and the insects assembled and sat down on one side of the plain, and the large animals were sitting on the other side of the plain.

and kill us and you!' and my brothers agreed. Therefore we have called you, and we tell you about our council." Thus spoke the Grizzly Bear. Moreover, he said, "Now I will ask you, large animals, is this so?"

Then the Panther spoke, and said, "I fully agree to this wise counsel," and all the large animals agreed. Then the Grizzly Bear turned to the small animals, who were seated on one side of the prairie, and said, "We want to know what you have to say in this matter." Then the small animals kept quiet, and did not reply to the question. After they had been silent for a while, one of their speakers, Porcupine, arose, and said, "Friends, let me say a word or two to answer your question. Your counsel is very good for yourselves, for you have plenty of warm fur, even for the most severe cold, but look down upon these little insects. They have no fur to warm themselves in winter; and how can small insects and other small animals obtain provisions if you ask for severe cold in winter? Therefore I say this, don't ask for the greatest cold." Then he stopped speaking and sat down.

Then Grizzly Bear arose, and said, "We will not pay any attention to what Porcupine says, for all the large animals agree." Therefore he turned his head toward the large animals, and said, "Did you agree when we asked for the severest cold on earth?" and all the large animals replied, "We all consented. We do not care for what Porcupine has said."

Then the same speaker arose again, and said, "Now, listen once more! I will ask you just one question." Thus spoke Porcupine: "How will you obtain plants to eat if you ask for very severe cold? And if it is so cold, the roots of all the wild berries will be withered and frozen, and all the plants of the prairie will wither away, owing to the frost of winter. How will you be able to get food? You are large animals, and you always walk about among the mountains wanting something to eat. Now, if your request is granted for severe cold every winter, you will die of starvation in spring or in summer; but we shall live, for we live on the bark of trees, and our smallest persons find their food in the gum of trees, and the smallest insects find their food in the earth."

After he had spoken, Porcupine put his thumb into his mouth and bit it off, and said, "Confound it!" and threw his thumb out of his mouth to show the large animals how clever he was, and sat down again, full of rage. Therefore the hand of the porcupine has only four fingers, no thumb.

All the large animals were speechless, because they wondered at the wisdom of Porcupine. Finally Grizzly Bear arose, and said, "It is true what you have said." Thus spoke Grizzly Bear to Porcupine, and all the large animals chose Porcupine to be their wise man and to be the first among all the small animals; and they all agreed that the cold in winter should be as much as it is now. They made six months for the winter and six months for summer.

Then Porcupine spoke again out of his wisdom, and said, "In winter we shall have ice and snow. In spring we shall have showers of rain, and the plants shall be green. In summer we shall have warmer weather, and all the fishes shall go up the rivers. In the fall the leaves shall fall; it shall rain, and the rivers and brooks shall overflow their banks. Then all the animals, large and small, and those that creep on the ground, shall go into their dens and hide themselves for six months." Thus spoke the wise Porcupine to all the animals. Then they all agreed to what Porcupine had proposed.

They all joyfully went to their own homes. Thus it happens that all the wild animals take to their dens in winter, and that all the large animals are in their dens in winter. Only Porcupine does not hide in a den in winter, but goes about visiting his neighbors, all the different kinds of animals that go to their dens, large animals as well as small ones.

The large animals refused the advice that Porcupine gave; and Porcupine was full of rage, went to those animals that had slighted him, and struck them with the quills of his tail, and the large animals were killed by them. Therefore all the animals are afraid of Porcupine to this day. That is the end.

The Story of Grizzly Bear and Beaver

(TSIMSHIAN)

THERE WAS a great lake close to Skeena River, where many beavers built their houses, because it was deep water and a safe hiding-place and good shelter for them in winter-time. There were many old houses, and new ones as well. They thought that their dangerous enemies could not reach them.

One day the beavers thought there was no danger near them. Therefore they left their houses and went out for fresh air, and they covered the melting ice. It was early in spring when the animals awoke from their winter sleep and came out of their dens. The Grizzly Bear had just come out from his winter sleep, and as soon as he came out he saw many beavers that covered the ice. He went there secretly, fell on them, and killed many of them. Some of them escaped to their houses in the lake; but the great Grizzly Bear hunted them to their houses, and slew many of them in their houses, and they were very sad. The great Grizzly Bear, however, was happy because he had much food, and the poor weak beavers were much distressed. He thought that these beavers would last him through the summer, and finally only one beaver escaped from his paws.

This poor Beaver went away down into the water, and the great Grizzly Bear was eating the beaver meat; and when he had enough, he lay down and slept among the slain beavers.

The poor lonely Beaver hid in the deep water and thought about her great enemy. Then she planned to make false ground on one side of the lake. So she took wet soft moss and put it at the butt end of a fallen tree which stretched over the water at one side of the great lake. She did so in the night, for she was afraid to work in the daytime. She made it look like dry land around the old fallen tree. At the end of the summer the salmon were in the creeks. Now, the great Grizzly Bear's beaver meat was all gone, and the great dreadful thing was very hungry. He was walking around the lake, searching for something to eat; and he went to the brooks and caught many salmon, which were to serve as his food in winter.

One day as he went about very hungry, walking about proudly, for he was stronger than any other animal, he stood there, and saw a poor weak Beaver sitting at the end of a fallen tree. She was sitting there very lonely. When the proud animal saw her sitting there, he asked with his proud voice, "What are you doing there, poor animal?" Thus said the proud Grizzly Bear when he saw her sitting on the end of an old log. The Beaver said, "Grizzly Bear shall die!" Then the Grizzly Bear became angry, and said, "Did you say I shall die?" but she did not even answer him. He walked down to and fro on the dry land at the foot of the fallen tree, on the end of which the poor little Beaver was sitting. The Beaver said again, "The great Grizzly Bear shall die!"— "Yes," said the great monster, "I will kill you right there. Don't run away! I will tear you right now!" and he walked toward the Beaver that was sitting there. He was walking along the log proudly, and said, "Don't run away! I will devour you!" but the brave Beaver replied, "Great Grizzly Bear shall die!"

Then the proud Grizzly Bear flew into a rage; but the poor Beaver remained sitting there, and then swam out into the water. Then she looked back at the Grizzly Bear, and said, "Grizzly Bear shall die!" At once the Grizzly Bear jumped on the Beaver, who dived under the fallen tree where she had made the false ground in order to entrap the great Grizzly Bear, and the great monster struggled in the slough that the Beaver had made. Then the Beaver came out on the surface and climbed on the log where she had been sitting before, and looked at the great Grizzly Bear who was struggling there. She said once more, "Grizzly Bear shall die!" The Grizzly Bear became tired out in the slough, and groaned in despair. He tried with all his might to get away, but he could not, because the soft mud and moss held him. He tried to swim, but he could not do it. When he was about to die, he said to the Beaver, "Come and help me!" and the Beaver said again, "Grizzly Bear shall die!" Now, the great animal howled and shouted and moaned and died there in despair. He was drowned in the slough, because he had no pity on the weak animals, and tried to devour all the weak animals. He thought there was no one besides himself. Yet the weak animal was stronger than he in wisdom, and the weak animal killed him. He was howling and crying,— he who had slain all the poor Beavers,—but no Beavers were crying or moaning when the great Grizzly Bear destroyed them. Therefore let not the strong oppress the poor or weak, for the weak shall have the victory over the mighty. This is the end.

How Master Lox as a Raccoon Killed the Bear and the Black Cats

(PASSAMAQUODDY)

ONE FINE morning Master Lox, who was a devilish spirit, started off as a Raccoon; for he walked the earth in diverse disguises, to take his usual roundabouts, and as he went he saw a huge bear, as the manuscript reads, "right straight ahead of him."

Now the old Bear was very glad to see the Raccoon, for he had made up his mind to kill him at once if he could: firstly, to punish him for his sins; and secondly, to eat him for breakfast. Then the Raccoon ran into a hollow tree, the Bear following, and beginning to root it up.

Now the Coon saw that in a few minutes the tree would go and he be gone. But he began to sing as if he did not care a bean, and said, "All the digging and pushing this tree will never catch me. Push your way in backwards, and then I must yield and die. But that you cannot do, since the hole is too small for you." Then Mooin, the Bruin, hearing this, believed it, but saw that he could easily enlarge the hole, which he did, and so put himself in arrear; upon which the Raccoon seized him, and held on till he was slain.

Then he crawled out of the tree, and, having made himself a fine pair of mittens out of the Bear's skin, started off again, and soon saw a wigwam from which rose a smoke, and, walking in, he found a family of *Begemkessisek*, or Black Cats. So, greeting them, he said, "Young folks, comb me down and make me nice, and I will give you these beautiful bear-skin mittens." So the little Black Cats combed him down, and parted his hair, and brushed his tail, and while they were doing this he fell asleep; and they, being very hungry, took the fresh bear-skin mitts, and scraped them all up, and cooked and ate them. Then the Coon, waking up, looked very angry at them, and said in an awful voice, "Where are my bear-skin mitts?" And they, in great fear, replied, "Please, sir, we cooked and ate them." Then the Coon flew at them and strangled them every one, all except the youngest, who, since he could not speak as yet, the Raccoon, or Lox, thought could not tell of him. Then, for a great joke, he took all the little dead creatures and set them up by the road-side in a row; as it was a cold day they all froze stiff, and then he put a stick across their jaws, so that the little Black Cats looked as if they were laughing for joy. Then he made off at full speed.

Soon the father, the old Black Cat, came home, and, seeing his children all grinning at him, he said, "How glad the dear little things are to see me." But as none moved he saw that something was wrong, and his joy soon changed to sorrow.

Then the youngest Black Cat, the baby, came out of some hole where he had hid himself. Now the baby was too young to speak, but he was very clever, and, picking up a piece of charcoal, he made a mark from the end of his mouth around his cheek. Then the father cried, "Ah, *now* I know who it was,— the Raccoon, as sure as I live!" And he started after him in hot pursuit.

Soon the Raccoon saw the fierce Black Cat, as an Indian, coming after him with a club. And, looking at him, he said, "No club can kill me; nothing but a bulrush or cat-tail can take my life." Then the Black Cat, who knew where to get one, galloped off to a swamp, and, having got a large cat-tail, came to the Coon and hit him hard with it. It burst and spread all over the Raccoon's head, and, being wet, the fuzz stuck to him. And the Black Cat, thinking it was the Coon's brains and all out, went his way.

The Raccoon lay quite still till his foe was gone, and then went on his travels. Now he was a great magician, though little to other folks' good. And he came to a place where there were many women nursing their babes, and said, "This is but a slow way you have of raising children." To which the good women replied, "How else should we raise them?" Then he answered, "I will show you how we do in our country. When we want them to grow fast, we dip them into cold water over night. Just lend me one, and I will show you how to raise them in a hurry." They gave him one: he took it to the river, and, cutting a hole in the ice, put the child into it. The next morning he went to the place, and took out a full-grown man, alive and well. The women were indeed astonished at this. All hastened to put their babes that night under the ice, and then the Raccoon rushed away. So they all died.

Then he came to another camp, where many women with fine stuff and furs were making bags. "That is a very slow way you have of working," he said to the goodwives. "In our country we cook them under the ashes. Let me see the stuff and show you how!" They gave him a piece: he put it under the hot coals and ashes, and in a few minutes drew out from them a beautiful bag. Then they all hurried to put their cloth under the fire. Just then he left in haste. And when they drew the stuff out it was scorched or burned, and all spoiled.

Then he came to a great river, and did not know how to get across. He saw on the bank an old *Wiwillmekq'*, a strange worm which is like a horned alligator; but he was blind. "Grandfather," said the Raccoon, "carry me over the lake." "Yes, my grandson," said the Wiwillmekq', and away he swam; the Ravens and Crows above began to ridicule them. "What are those birds saying?" inquired the Old One. "Oh, they are crying to you to hurry, hurry, for your life, with that Raccoon!" So the Wiwillmekq', not seeing land ahead, hurried with such speed that the Raccoon made him run his head and half his body into the bank, and then jumped off and left him. But whether the Wiwillmekq' ever got out again is more than he ever troubled himself to know.

So he went on till he came to some Black Berries, and said, "Berries, how would you agree with me if I should eat you?" "Badly indeed, Master Coon," they replied, "for we are Choke-berries." "Choke-berries, indeed! Then I will have none of you." And then further he found on some bushes, Rice-berries. "Berries," he cried, "how would you agree with me if I should eat you?" "We should make you itch, for we are Itch-berries." "Ah, that is what I like," he replied, and so ate his fill. Then as he went on he felt very uneasy: he seemed to be tormented with prickles, he scratched and scratched, but it did not help or cure. So he rubbed himself on a ragged rock; he slid up and down it till the hair came off.

Now the Raccoon is bare or has little fur where he scratched himself, to this very day. This story is at an end.

The Ants That Pushed on the Sky

(PUEBLO)

ONCE UPON a time there lived in one of the prehistoric pueblos east of the Manzano Mountains a young Indian named Kahp-too-óo-yoo, the Corn-stalk Young Man. He was not only a famous hunter and a brave warrior against the raiding Comanches, but a great wizard; and to him the Trues had given the power of the clouds. When Kahp-too-óo-yoo willed it, the glad rains fell, and made the dry fields laugh in green; and without him no one could bring water from the sky. His father was Old-Black-Cane, his mother was Corn-Woman, and his two sisters were Yellow-Corn-Maiden, and Blue-Corn-Maiden.

Kahp-too-óo-yoo had a friend, a young man of about the same age. But, as is often true, the friend was of a false heart, and was really a witch, though Kahp-too-óo-yoo never dreamed of such a thing.

The two young men used to go together to the mountains to get wood, and always carried their bows and arrows, to kill deer and antelopes, or whatever game they might find.

One day the false friend came to Kahp-too-óo-yoo, and said:

"Friend, let us go to-morrow for wood, and to hunt."

They agreed that so they would do. Next day they started before sunrise, and came presently to the spot where they gathered wood. Just there they started a herd of deer. Kahp-too-óo-yoo followed part of the herd, which fled to the northwest, and the friend pursued those that went southwest. After a long, hard chase, Kahp-too-óo-yoo killed a deer with his swift arrows, and brought it on his strong back to the place where they had separated. Presently came the friend, very hot and tired, and with empty hands; and seeing the deer, he was pinched with jealousy.

"Come, friend," said Kahp-too-óo-yoo. "It is well for brothers to share with brothers. Take of this deer and cook and eat; and carry a part to your house, as if you had killed it yourself."

"Thank you," answered the other coldly, as one who will not; but he did not accept.

When they had gathered each a load of wood, and lashed it with rawhide thongs in bundles upon their shoulders, they trudged home—Kahp-too-óo-yoo carrying the deer on top of his wood. His sisters received him with joy, praising him as a hunter; and the friend went away to his house, with a heavy face.

Several different days when they went to the mountain together, the very same thing came to pass. Kahp-too-óo-yoo killed each time a deer; and each time the friend came home with nothing, refusing all offers to share as brothers. And he grew more jealous and more sullen every day.

At last he came again to invite Kahp-too-óo-yoo to go; but this time it was with an evil purpose that he asked. Then again the same things happened. Again the unsuccessful friend refused to take a share of Kahp-too-óo-yoo's deer; and when he had sat long without a word, he said:

"Friend Kahp-too-óo-yoo, now I will prove you if you are truly my friend, for I do not think it."

"Surely," said Kahp-too-óo-yoo, "if there is any way to prove myself, I will do it gladly, for truly I am your friend."

"Then come, and we will play a game together, and with that I will prove you."

"It is well! But what game shall we play, for here we have nothing?"

Near them stood a broken pine-tree, with one great arm from its twisted body. And looking at it, the false friend said:

"I see nothing but to play the *gallo* race; and because we have no horses we will ride this arm of the pine-tree—first I will ride, and then you."

So he climbed the pine-tree, and sat astride the limb as upon a horse, and rode, reaching over to the ground as if to pick up the chicken.

"Now you," he said, coming down; and Kahp-too-óo-yoo climbed the tree and rode on the swinging branch. But the false friend bewitched the pine, and suddenly it grew in a moment to the very sky, carrying Kahp-too-óo-yoo.

"We do this to one another," taunted the false friend, as the tree shot up; and taking the wood, and the deer which Kahp-too-óo-yoo had killed, he went to the village. There the sisters met him, and asked:

"Where is our brother?"

"Truly I know not, for he went northwest and I southwest; and though I waited long at the meeting-place, he did not come. Probably he will soon return. But take of this deer which I killed, for sisters should share the labors of brothers."

But the girls would take no meat, and went home sorrowful.

Time went on, and still there was no Kahp-too-óo-yoo. His sisters and his old parents wept always, and all the village was sad. And soon the crops grew yellow in the fields, and the springs failed, and the animals walked like weary shadows; for Kahp-too-óo-yoo, he who had the power of the clouds, was gone, and there was no rain. And then perished all that is green; the animals fell in the brown fields; and the gaunt people who sat to warm themselves in the sun began to die there where they sat. At last the poor old man said to his daughters:

"Little daughters, prepare food, for again we will go to look for your brother."

The girls made cakes of the blue corn-meal for the journey; and on the fourth day they started. Old-Black-Cane hobbled to the south, his wife to the east, the elder girl to the north, and the younger to the west.

For a great distance they traveled; and at last Blue-Corn-Maiden, who was in the north, heard a far, faint song. It was so little that she thought it must be imaginary; but she stopped to listen, and softly, softly it came again:

> *Tó-ai-fóo-ni-hlóo-hlim,*
> *Eng-k'hai k'háhm;*
> *Eé-eh-bóori-kóon-hlee-oh,*
> *Ing-k'hai k'háhm.*
> *Ah-ee-ái, ah-hee-ái,*
> *Aim!*

(Old-Black-Cane
My father is called;
Corn-Woman
My mother is called.
*Ah-ee-ái, ah-hee-ái,
Aim!*)

When she heard this, Blue-Corn-Maiden ran until she came to her sister, and cried:

"Sister! Sister! I think I hear our brother somewhere in captivity. Listen!"

Trembling, they listened; and again the song came floating to them, so soft, so sad that they wept—as to this day their people weep when a white-haired old man, filled with the memories of Kahp-too-óo-yoo, sings that plaintive melody.

"Surely it is our brother!" they cried; and off they went running to find their parents. And when all listened together, again they heard the song.

"Oh, my son!" cried the poor old woman, "in what captivity do you find yourself? True it is that your father is Old-Black-Cane, and I, your mother, am called Corn-Woman. But why do you sing thus?"

Then all four of them began to follow the song, and at last they came to the foot of the sky-reaching pine; but they could see nothing of Kahp-too-óo-yoo, nor could their cries reach him. There, on the ground, were his bow and arrows, with strings and feathers eaten away by time; and there was his pack of wood, tied with the rawhide thong, ready to be taken home. But after they had searched everywhere, they could not find Kahp-too-óo-yoo; and finally they went home heavy at heart.

At last it happened that P'ah-whá-yoo-óo-deh, the Little Black Ant, took a journey and went up the bewitched pine, even to its top in the sky. When he found Kahp-too-óo-yoo there a prisoner, the Little Black Ant was astonished, and said:

"Great *Kah-báy-deh* [Man of Power], how comes it that you are up here in such a condition, while your people at home are suffering and dying for rain, and few are left to meet you if you return? Are you here of your free will?"

"No," groaned Kahp-too-óo-yoo; "I am here because of the jealousy of him who was as my brother, with whom I shared my food and labor, whose home was my home, and my home his. He is the cause, for he was jealous and bewitched me hither. And now I am dying of famine."

"If that is so," said the Little Black Ant, "I will be the one to help you"; and he ran down to the world as fast as he could. When he got there he sent out the crier to summon all his nation, and also that of the *In-toon*, the Big Red Ants. Soon all the armies of the Little

Soon all the armies of the Little Black Ants and
the Big Red Ants met at the foot of the pine, and
held a council.

Black Ants and the Big Red Ants met at the foot of the pine, and held a council. They smoked the *weer* and deliberated what should be done.

"You Big Red Ants are stronger than we who are small," said the War-Captain of the Little Black Ants, "and for that you ought to take the top of the tree to work."

"Een-dah!" (No) said the War-Captain of the Big Red Ants. "If you think we are the stronger, give us the bottom, where we can work more, and you go to the top."

So it was agreed, and the captains made their armies ready. But first the Little Black Ants got the cup of an acorn, and mixed in it corn-meal and water and honey, and carried it up the tree. They were so many that they covered its trunk all the way to the sky.

When Kahp-too-óo-yoo saw, his heart was heavy, and he thought: "But what good will that very little do me, for I am dying of hunger and thirst?"

"Nay, friend," answered the Captain of the Little Black Ants, who knew his thought. "A person should not think so. This little is enough, and there will be some left."

And it was so; for when Kahp-too-óo-yoo had eaten all he could, the acorn-cup was still nearly full. Then the ants carried the cup to the ground and came back to him.

"Now, friend," said the Captain, "we will do our best. But now you must shut your eyes till I say '*Ahw!*' "

Kahp-too-óo-yoo shut his eyes, and the Captain sent signals down to those at the foot of the tree. And the Little Black Ants above put their feet against the sky and pushed with all their might on the top of the pine; and the Big Red Ants below caught the trunk and pulled as hard as they could; and the very first tug drove the great pine a quarter of its length into the earth.

"*Ahw!*" shouted the Captain of the Little Black Ants, and Kahp-too-óo-yoo opened his eyes; but he could see nothing below.

"Shut your eyes again," said the Captain, giving the signal. Again the Little Black Ants pushed mightily against the sky, and the Big Red Ants pulled mightily from below; and the pine was driven another fourth of its length into the earth.

"*Ahw!*" cried the Captain; and when Kahp-too-óo-yoo opened his eyes he could just see the big, brown world.

Again he closed his eyes. There was another great push and pull, and only a quarter of the pine was left above the ground. Now Kahp-too-óo-yoo could see, far below, the parched fields strewn with dead animals, and his own village full of dying people.

Again the Little Black Ants pushed and the Big Red Ants pulled, and this time the tree was driven clear out of sight, and Kahp-too-óo-yoo was left sitting on the ground. He hastily made a bow and arrows and soon killed a fat deer, which he brought and divided among the Little Black Ants and the Big Red Ants, thanking them for their kindness.

Then he made all his clothing to be new, for he had been four years a prisoner in the bewitched tree, and was all in rags. Making for himself a flute from the bark of a young tree, he played upon it as he strode homeward and sang:

> *Kahp-too-óo-yoo tú-mah-quee,*
> *Nah-chóor kwé-shay-tin,*
> *Nah-shúr kwé-shay-tin;*
> *Kahp-too-óo-yoo tú-mah-quee!*
>
> (Kahp-too-óo-yoo has come to life again,
> Is back to his home coming,
> Blowing the yellow and the blue;
> Kahp-too-óo-yoo has come to life again!)

As he walked and sang, the forgotten clouds came over him, and the soft rain began to fall, and all was green and good. But only so far as his voice reached came the rain; and beyond all was still death and drought. When he came to the end of the wet, he played and sang again; and again the rain fell as far as his voice was heard. This time the Fool-Boy, who was wandering outside the dying village, saw the far storm and heard the singing. He ran to tell Kahp-too-óo-yoo's parents; but nobody would believe a Foolish, and they sent him away.

When the Fool-Boy went out again, the rain fell on him and gave him strength, and he came running a second time to tell. Then the sisters came out of the house and saw the rain and heard the song; and they cried for joy, and told their parents to rise and meet him. But the poor old people were dying of weakness, and could not rise; and the sisters went alone. When they met him they fell on their knees, weeping; but Kahp-too-óo-yoo lifted them up and blessed them, gave an ear of blue corn to Blue-Corn-Maiden, and to Yellow-Corn-Maiden an ear of yellow corn, and brought them home.

As he sang again, the rain fell in the village; and when it touched the pinched faces of the dead they sat up and opened their mouths to catch it. And the dying crawled out to drink, and were strong again; and the withered fields grew green and glad.

When they came to the house, Kahp-too-óo-yoo blessed his parents, and then said:

"Little sisters, give us to eat."

But they answered, "How? For you have been gone these four years, and there was none to give us rain. We planted, but nothing came, and to-day we ate the last grain."

"Nay, little sisters," he said. "A person should not think so. Look now in the store-rooms, if there be not something there."

"But we have looked and looked, and turned over everything to try to find one grain."

"Yet look once more," he said; and when they opened the door, there was the store-room piled to the roof with corn, and another room was full of wheat. Then they cried for joy, and began to roast the blue ears, for they were dying of hunger.

At the sweet smell of the roasting corn came the starving neighbors, crowding at the door, and crying:

"O Kahp-too-óo-yoo! Give us to taste one grain of corn, and then we will go home and die."

But Kahp-too-óo-yoo handed to each an ear, and said:

"Fathers, brothers, go now to your own houses, for there you will find corn as much as here." And when they went, it was so. All began to roast corn and to eat; and the dead in the houses awoke and were strong again, and all the village sang and danced.

From that time there was plenty of rain, for

he who had the power of the clouds was at home again. In the spring the people planted, and in the fall the crops were so great that all the town could not hold them; so that which was left they brought to Shee-eh-whíb-bak (Isleta), where we enjoy it to this day.

As for the false friend, he died of shame in his house, not daring to come out; and no one wept for him.

The Little Boy Man

(SIOUX)

AT THE beginning of things, He-who-was-first-Created found himself living alone. The earth was here before him, clothed in green grass and thick forests, and peopled with the animal tribes. Then all these spoke one language, and the Lonely One was heralded by them everywhere as he roamed to and fro over the world, both upon dry land and in the depths of the sea.

One day, when he returned to his teepee from a long wandering, he felt a pain in his left foot, and discovered a splinter in the great toe! Drawing out the splinter, he tossed it upward through the smoke-hole of the lodge. He could hear it roll and rattle down over the birch-bark covering, and in the instant that it touched the ground, there arose the cry of a new-born child!

He-who-was-first-Created at once came forth and took up the infant, who was the Boy Man, the father of the human race here upon earth.

Now the little Boy Man grew and flourished, and was perfectly happy under the wise guidance of his friend and Elder Brother. Although he had neither father nor mother, and only animals for playmates, it is said that no child born of human parents has ever led so free and happy a life as he. In those days, there was peace between the animals and the Boy Man. Sometimes they challenged him to friendly contests, whereupon He-who-was-first-Created taught his little brother how to outwit them by clever tricks and devices. This he was often able to do; but not always; for sometimes the animals by their greater strength finally overcame him.

One morning the Boy Man went out from his lodge as usual to the day's occupations, but did not return at night nor for many nights afterward. He-who-was-first-Created mourned and wailed long for the lost one. At last he became angry, and set out to look for the bones of his brother.

He travelled from east to west across the world, but found no trace of the one he sought, and all of the land creatures whom he questioned declared that they had not seen him pass by.

Next he followed the rivers, and the shores of the Great Lakes, and there one day he heard an old woman singing as she cut down a tree at the edge of the water. The traveller came closer to hear the words of the song. It was a song of the scalp-dance, and in it she spoke the name of the lost Boy Man.

He-who-was-first-Created now turned himself into a King-fisher, and so approached unsuspected and talked with the old Beaver-woman. From her he learned that his younger brother had been enticed into the Great Water and destroyed by the monster of the deep, Unk-tay-hee. Thereupon he went down to the shore and changed himself into a tall pine overlooking the lake.

For many moons He-who-was-first-Created remained thus, until at last he beheld two huge forms rising up in the midst of the waves. The monsters glided gradually toward the shore and lay basking in the sun at his feet, rocking gently with the motion of the quiet water. It was old Unk-tay-hee and his mate.

"Husband!" exclaimed the wife of Unk-tay-hee, "for ages this has been our resting-place, and yet I have never seen this tree before!"

"Woman, the tree has always been there!" returned the water monster.

"But I am sure it was not here before," she insisted.

Then Unk-tay-hee wound his immense scaly

tail about the giant pine and tried to pull it out by the roots. The water foamed and boiled with his struggles, but He-who-was-first-Created stood firm, and at last the monster gave up the attempt.

"There," he declared, "I told you it had always been there!" His wife appeared satisfied, and presently the gentle waves rocked them both to sleep.

Then He-who-was-first-Created returned to his own shape, and with his long spear he stabbed each of the monsters, so that with groans of pain they dove down to their homes at the bottom of the great lake, and the waters boiled above them, and the foam was red with their blood.

The Daughter of the Sun

(CHEROKEE)

THE SUN lived on the other side of the sky vault, but her daughter lived in the middle of the sky, directly above the earth, and every day as the Sun was climbing along the sky arch to the west she used to stop at her daughter's house for dinner.

Now, the Sun hated the people on the earth, because they could never look straight at her without screwing up their faces. She said to her brother, the Moon, "My grandchildren are ugly; they grin all over their faces when they look at me." But the Moon said, "I like my younger brothers; I think they are very handsome"—because they always smiled pleasantly when they saw him in the sky at night, for his rays were milder.

The Sun was jealous and planned to kill all the people, so every day when she got near her daughter's house she sent down such sultry rays that there was a great fever and the people died by hundreds, until everyone had lost some friend and there was fear that no one would be left. They went for help to the

Little Men, who said the only way to save themselves was to kill the Sun.

The Little Men made medicine and changed two men to snakes, the Spreading-adder and the Copperhead, and sent them to watch near the door of the daughter of the Sun to bite the old Sun when she came next day. They went together and hid near the house until the Sun came, but when the Spreading-adder was about to spring, the bright light blinded him and he could only spit out yellow slime, as he does to this day when he tries to bite. She called him a nasty thing and went by into the house, and the Copperhead crawled off without trying to do anything.

So the people still died from the heat, and they went to the Little Men a second time for help. The Little Men made medicine again and changed one man into the great Uktena and another into the Rattlesnake and sent them to watch near the house and kill the old Sun when she came for dinner. They made the Uktena very large, with horns on his head, and everyone thought he would be sure to do the work, but the Rattlesnake was so quick and eager that he got ahead and coiled up just outside the house, and when the Sun's daughter opened the door to look out for her mother, he sprang up and bit her and she fell

dead in the doorway. He forgot to wait for the
old Sun, but went back to the people, and the
Uktena was so very angry that he went back,
too. Since then we pray to the rattlesnake and
do not kill him, because he is kind and never
tries to bite if we do not disturb him. The
Uktena grew angrier all the time and very
dangerous, so that if he even looked at a man,
that man's family would die. After a long time
the people held a council and decided that he
was too dangerous to be with them, so they
sent him up to Gălûñ′lătĭ, and he is there now.
The Spreading-adder, the Copperhead, the
Rattlesnake, and the Uktena were all men.

When the Sun found her daughter dead, she
went into the house and grieved, and the people did not die any more, but now the world
was dark all the time, because the Sun would
not come out. They went again to the Little
Men, and these told them that if they wanted
the Sun to come out again they must bring
back her daughter from Tsûsginâ′ĭ, the Ghost
country, in Usûñhi′yĭ, the Darkening land in
the west. They chose seven men to go, and
gave each a sourwood rod a hand-breadth
long. The Little Men told them they must take
a box with them, and when they got to
Tsûsginâ′ĭ they would find all the ghosts at a
dance. They must stand outside the circle,

The young woman was in the outside circle.

and when the young woman passed in the dance they must strike her with the rods and she would fall to the ground. Then they must put her into the box and bring her back to her mother, but they must be very sure not to open the box, even a little way, until they were home again.

They took the rods and a box and traveled seven days to the west until they came to the Darkening land. There were a great many people there, and they were having a dance just as if they were at home in the settlements. The young woman was in the outside circle, and as she swung around to where the seven men were standing, one struck her with his rod and she turned her head and saw him. As she came around the second time another touched her with his rod, and then another and another, until at the seventh round she fell out of the ring, and they put her into the box and closed the lid fast. The other ghosts seemed never to notice what had happened.

They took up the box and started home toward the east. In a little while the girl came to life again and begged to be let out of the box, but they made no answer and went on. Soon she called again and said she was hungry, but still they made no answer and went on. After another while she spoke again and called for a drink and pleaded so that it was very hard to listen to her, but the men who carried the box said nothing and still went on. When at last they were very near home, she called again and begged them to raise the lid just a little, because she was smothering. They were afraid she was really dying now, so they lifted the lid a little to give her air, but as they did so there was a fluttering sound inside and something flew past them into the thicket and they heard a redbird cry, *"kwish! kwish! kwish!"* in the bushes. They shut down the lid and went on again to the settlements, but when they got there and opened the box it was empty.

So we know the Redbird is the daughter of the Sun, and if the men had kept the box closed, as the Little Men told them to do, they would have brought her home safely, and we could bring back our other friends also from the Ghost country, but now when they die we can never bring them back.

The Sun had been glad when they started to the Ghost country, but when they came back without her daughter she grieved and cried, "My daughter, my daughter," and wept until her tears made a flood upon the earth, and the people were afraid the world would be drowned. They held another council, and sent their handsomest young men and women to amuse her so that she would stop crying. They danced before the Sun and sang their best songs, but for a long time she kept her face covered and paid no attention, until at last the drummer suddenly changed the song, when she lifted up her face, and was so pleased at the sight that she forgot her grief and smiled.

The Girl Who Married the Star

(SIOUX)

THERE WERE once two sisters who lived alone in an uninhabited place. This was a long time ago, when the tribes upon earth were few, and the animal people were friendly to man. The name of one of the girls was Earth, and the other was called Water.

All their food was brought to them by their animal friends. The Bears supplied them with nuts, berries and wild turnips, and the Bees brought combs dripping with honey. They ate no flesh, for that would be to take life. They dwelt in a lodge made of birch-bark, and their beds were mats woven of rushes.

One clear, summer night the girls lay awake upon their beds, looking up through the smoke-hole of their wigwam and telling one another all their thoughts.

"Sister," said the Earth, "I have seen a handsome young man in my dreams, and it seemed to me that he came from up yonder!"

"I too have seen a man in my dreams," replied her sister, "and he was a great brave."

"Do you not think these bright stars above

us are the sky men of whom we have dreamed?" suggested the Earth.

"If that is true, sister, and it may be true," said the Water, "I choose that brightest Star for my husband!"

"And I," declared her sister, "choose for my husband that little twinkling Star!"

By and by the sisters slept; and when they awoke, they found themselves in the sky! The husband of the elder sister who had chosen the bright star was an old warrior with a shining name, but the husband of the younger girl was a fine-looking young man, who had as yet no great reputation.

The Star men were kind to their wives, who lived very happily in their new home. One day they went out to dig wild turnips, and the old warrior said to his wife:

"When you are digging, you must not hit the ground too hard!"

The younger man also warned his wife, saying:

"Do not hit the ground too hard!"

However, the Earth forgot, and in her haste she struck the ground so hard with the sharp-pointed stick with which she dug turnips, that the floor of the sky was broken and she fell through.

Two very old people found the poor girl lying in the meadow.

They kindly made for her a little wigwam of pine boughs, and brought ferns for her bed. The old woman nursed her as well as she could, but she did nothing but wail and cry.

"Let me go to him!" she begged. "I cannot live without my husband!"

Night came, and the stars appeared in the sky as usual. Only the little twinkling Star did not appear, for he was now a widower and had painted his face quite black.

The poor wife waited for him a long time, but he did not come, because he could not. At last she slept, and dreamed she saw a tiny red Star in the sky that had not been there before.

"Ah!" said she, "that is Red Star, my son!"

In the morning she found at her side a pretty little boy, a Star Boy, who afterward grew to be a handsome young man and had many adventures. His guides by night through the pathless woods were the Star children of his mother's sister, his cousins in the sky.

The Man Who Married the Moon

(ISLETA PUEBLO)

LONG BEFORE the first Spaniards came to New Mexico, Isleta stood where it stands to-day—on a lava ridge that defies the gnawing current of the Rio Grande. In those far days, Nah-chu-rú-chu, "The Bluish Light of Dawn," dwelt in Isleta, and was a leader of his people. A weaver by trade, his rude loom hung from the dark rafters of his room; and in it he wove the strong black mantas or robes like those which are the dress of Pueblo women to this day.

Besides being very wise in medicine, Nah-chu-rú-chu was young, and tall, and strong, and handsome. All the girls of the village thought it a shame that he did not care to take a wife. For him the shyest dimples played, for him the whitest teeth flashed out, as the owners passed him in the plaza; but he had no eyes for them. Then, in the custom of the Tiwa, bashful fingers worked wondrous fringed shirts of buckskin, or gay awl-sheaths, which found their way to his house by unknown messengers.

59

But Nah-chu-rú-chu paid no more attention to the gifts than to the smiles, and just kept weaving and weaving—such mantas as were never seen in the land of the Tiwa before or since.

Two of his admirers were sisters who were called, in Tiwa language, Ee-eh-chóo-ri-ch'áhm-nin—the Yellow-Corn-Maidens. They were both young and pretty, but they "had the evil road," or were witches, possessed of a magic power which they always used for ill. When all the other girls gave up, discouraged at Nah-chu-rú-chu's indifference, the Yellow-Corn-Maidens kept coming day after day, trying to win his notice. At last the matter became so annoying to Nah-chu-rú-chu that he hired the deep-voiced town crier to go through all the streets and announce that in four days Nah-chu-rú-chu would choose a wife.

For dippers to take water from the big earthen jars, the Tiwa used then, as they use to-day, queer little *omates* made of a gourd. But Nah-chu-rú-chu, being a great medicine-man and very rich, had a dipper of pure pearl, shaped like the gourds, but wonderfully precious.

"On the fourth day," proclaimed the crier, "Nah-chu-rú-chu will hang his pearl *omate* at his door, when every girl who will may throw a handful of corn-meal at it. And she whose meal is so well ground that it sticks to the *omate*, she shall be the wife of Nah-chu-rú-chu!"

When this strange news came rolling down the still evening air, there was a great scampering of little moccasined feet. The girls ran out from hundreds of gray adobe houses to catch every word; and when the crier had passed on, they ran back into the store-rooms and began to ransack the corn-bins for the biggest, evenest, and most perfect ears. Shelling the choicest, each took her few handfuls of kernels to the sloping *metate*, and with the *mano*, or hand-stone, scrubbed the blue grist up and down and up and down till the hard corn was a soft blue meal. All the next day, and the next, and the next, they ground it over and over again, until it grew finer than ever flour was before; and every girl felt sure that her meal would stick to the *omate* of the handsome young weaver. The Yellow-Corn-Maidens worked hardest of all; day and night for four days they ground and ground, with all the magic spells they knew.

Now, in those far-off days the Moon had not gone into the sky to live, but was a maiden of Isleta. And a very beautiful girl she was, but blind of one eye. She had long admired Nah-chu-rú-chu, but was always too maidenly to try to attract his attention as the other girls had done; and at the time when the crier made his proclamation, she happened to be away at her father's ranch. It was only upon the fourth day that she returned to town, and in a few moments the girls were to go with their meal to test it upon the magic dipper. The two Yellow-Corn-Maidens were just coming from their house as she passed, and they told her what was to be done. They were very confident of success, and hoped to hurt her. They laughed derisively as she went running to her home.

By this time a long file of girls was coming to Nah-chu-rú-chu's house, outside whose door hung the pearl *omate*. Each girl carried in her hand a little jar of meal. As they passed the door, one by one, each took from the jar a handful and threw it against the magic dipper. But each time the meal dropped to the ground, and left the pure pearl undimmed and radiant as ever.

At last came the Yellow-Corn-Maidens, who had waited to watch the failure of the others. As they came where they could see Nah-chu-rú-chu sitting at his loom, they called: "Ah! here we have the meal that will stick!" and each threw a handful at the *omate*. But it did not stick at all; and still from his seat Nah-chu-rú-chu could see, in the shell's mirror-like surface, all that went on outside.

The Yellow-Corn-Maidens were very angry, and instead of passing on as the others had done, they stood there and kept throwing and throwing at the *omate*, which smiled back at them with undiminished luster.

Just then, last of all, came the Moon, with a single handful of meal which she had hastily ground. The two sisters were in a fine rage by this time, and mocked her, saying:

"Hoh! P'áh-hlee-oh, Moon, you poor thing, we are very sorry for you! Here we have been grinding our meal for four days and still it will not stick, and we did not tell you till to-day. How then can you ever hope to win Nah-chu-rú-chu? Puh, you silly little thing!"

But the Moon paid no attention whatsoever to their taunts. Drawing back her little dimpled hand, she threw the meal gently against the pearl *omate*, and so fine was it ground that every tiniest bit of it clung to the polished shell, and not a particle fell to the ground!

When Nah-chu-rú-chu saw that, he rose up quickly from his loom and came and took the Moon by the hand, saying: "You are she who

She threw the meal gently against the pearl *omate*.

shall be my wife. You shall never want for anything, since I have very much." And he gave her many beautiful mantas, and cotton wraps, and fat boots of buckskin that wrap round and round, that she might dress as the wife of a rich chief. But the Yellow-Corn-Maidens, who had seen it all, went away vowing vengeance on the Moon.

Nah-chu-rú-chu and his sweet Moon-wife were very happy together. There was no other such housekeeper in all the pueblo as she, and no other hunter brought home so much buffalo-meat from the vast plains to the east, nor so many antelopes, and black-tailed deer, and jack-rabbits from the Manzanos, as did Nah-chu-rú-chu. But constantly he was saying to her:

"Moon-wife, beware of the Yellow-Corn-Maidens, for they have the evil road and will try to do you harm; but you must always refuse to do whatever they propose."

And always the young wife promised.

One day the Yellow-Corn-Maidens came to the house and said: "Friend Nah-chu-rú-chu, we are going to the llano, the plain, to gather amole." (Amole is a soapy root the Pueblos use for washing.) "Will you not let your wife go with us?"

"Oh, yes, she may go," said Nah-chu-rú-chu.

But taking her aside, he said: "Now be sure that while you are with them, you refuse whatever they may propose."

The Moon promised, and started away with the Yellow-Corn-Maidens.

In those days there was only a thick forest of cottonwoods where now the smiling vineyards, gardens, and orchards of Isleta are spread, and to reach the llano the three women had to go through the forest. In the very center of it they came to a deep *pozo*—a square well, with steps at one side leading down to the water's edge.

"Ay!" said the Yellow-Corn-Maidens, "How hot and thirsty is our walk! Come, let us get a drink of water."

But the Moon, remembering her husband's words, said politely that she did not wish to drink. They urged in vain, but at last, looking down into the *pozo*, they called:

"Oh, Moon-friend, Moon-friend! Come and look in this still water, and see how pretty you are!"

The Moon, you must know, has always been just as fond of looking at herself in the water as she is to this very day; and forgetting Nah-chu-rú-chu's warning, she came to the brink and looked down upon her fair reflection. But at that very moment the two witch-sisters pushed her head foremost into the *pozo*, and drowned her; and then they filled the well with earth, and went away as happy as wicked hearts can be.

As the sun crept along the adobe floor, closer and closer to his seat, Nah-chu-rú-chu began to look oftener from his loom to the door. When the shadows were very long, he sprang suddenly to his feet, and walked to the house of the Yellow-Corn-Maidens with long, long strides.

"Yellow-Corn-Maidens," he asked them very sternly, "where is my little wife?"

"Why, isn't she at home?" asked the wicked sisters, as if greatly surprised. "She got enough amole long before we did."

"Ah," groaned Nah-chu-rú-chu within himself, "it is as I thought—they have done her ill."

But without a word to them he turned on his heel and went away.

From that hour all went wrong at Isleta; for Nah-chu-rú-chu held the well-being of all his people, even unto life and death. Paying no attention to what was going on about him, he sat motionless upon the topmost crosspiece of the *estufa* (the kiva, or sacred council chamber ladder—the highest point in all the town) with his head bowed upon his hands.

There he sat for days, never speaking, never moving. The children who played along the streets looked up with awe to the motionless figure, and ceased their boisterous play. The old men shook their heads gravely, and muttered: "We are in evil times, for Nah-chu-rú-chu is mourning and will not be comforted; and there is no more rain, so that our crops are dying in the fields. What shall we do?"

At last all the councilors met together, and decided that there must be another effort made to find the lost wife. It was true that the great Nah-chu-rú-chu had searched for her in vain, and the people had helped him; but perhaps someone else might be more fortunate. So they took some of the sacred smoking-weed wrapped in a corn-husk and went to the Eagle, who has the sharpest eyes in all the world. Giving him the sacred gift, they said:

"Eagle-friend, we see Nah-chu-rú-chu in great trouble, for he has lost his Moon-wife. Come, search for her, we pray you, to discover if she be alive or dead."

So the Eagle took the offering, and smoked the smoke-prayer; and then he went winging upward into the sky. Higher and higher he rose, in great upward circles, while his keen eyes noted every stick, and stone, and animal on the face of all the world. But with all his eyes, he could see nothing of the lost wife; and at last he came back sadly, and said:

"People-friends, I went up to where I could see the whole world, but I could not find her."

Then the people went with an offering to the Coyote, whose nose is sharpest in all the world, and besought him to try and find the Moon. The Coyote smoked the smoke-prayer, and started off with his nose to the ground, trying to find her tracks. He trotted all over the earth; but at last he too came back without finding what he sought.

Then the troubled people got the Badger to search, for he is the best of all the beasts at digging (it was he whom the Trues employed to dig the caves in which the people first dwelt when they came to this world). The Badger trotted and pawed, and dug everywhere, but he could not find the Moon; and he came home very sad.

Then they asked the Osprey, who can see furthest under water, and he sailed high above the lakes and rivers in the world, till he could count the pebbles and the fish in them, but he too failed to discover the lost Moon.

By this time the crops were dead and sere in the fields, and thirsty animals walked crying along the river. Scarcely could the people themselves dig deep enough to find water to keep them alive. They were at a loss, but at last they thought: We will go now to the P'ah-kú-ee-teh-áy-deh (the "water-goose grandfather," which means Turkey-buzzard), who can find the dead—for surely she is dead, or the others would have found her.

So they went to him, and besought him. The Turkey-buzzard wept when he saw Nah-chu-rú-chu still sitting there upon the ladder, and said: "Truly it is sad for our great friend; but for me, I am afraid to go, since they who are more mighty than I have already failed. Yet I will try." And spreading his broad wings, he went climbing up the spiral ladder of the sky. Higher he wheeled, and higher, till at last not even the Eagle could see him. Up and up, till the sun began to singe his head, and not even the Eagle had ever been so high. He cried with pain, but still he kept mounting—until he was so close to the sun that all the feathers were burned from his head and neck. But he could see nothing, and at last, frantic with the burning, he came wheeling downward. When he got back to the *estufa* where all the people were waiting, they saw that his head and neck had been burned bare of feathers—and from that day to this the feathers would never grow out again.

"And did you see nothing?" they all asked, when they had bathed his burns.

"Nothing," he answered, "except that when I was halfway down, I saw in the middle of yon cottonwood forest a little mound covered with all the beautiful flowers in the world."

"Oh!" cried Nah-chu-rú-chu, speaking for the first time, "Go, friend, and bring me one flower from the very middle of the mound."

Off flew the Buzzard, and in a few minutes returned with a little white flower. Nah-chu-rú-chu took it and, descending from the ladder in silence, walked solemnly to his house, while all the wondering people followed.

When Nah-chu-rú-chu came inside his home once more, he took a new manta and spread it in the middle of the room. Laying the wee white flower tenderly in its center, he put another manta above it. Then, dressing himself in the splendid buckskin suit that the lost wife had made him, and taking in his right hand the sacred *guaje*, rattle, he seated himself at the head of the mantas and sang:

"*Shú-nah, shú-nah! Aí-ay-ay, aí-ay-ay, ai-ay-ay!* Seeking her, seeking her! There-away, there-away!"

When he had finished the song, all could see that the flower had begun to grow, so that it lifted the upper manta a little. Again he sang, shaking his gourd; and still the flower kept growing. Again and again he sang; and when he had finished for the fourth time, it was plain to all that a human form lay between the two mantas. And when he sang his song the fifth time, the form sat up and moved. Tenderly he lifted away the upper cloth; and there sat his sweet Moon-wife, fairer than ever, and alive as before!

For four days the people danced and sang in the public square. Nah-chu-rú-chu was happy again; and now the rain began to fall. The choked earth drank and was glad and green, and the dead crops came to life.

When his wife told him what the witch sisters had done, he was very angry; and that day he made a beautiful hoop to play the hoop game. He painted it, and put many strings across it, and decorated it with beaded buckskin.

"Now," said he, "the wicked Yellow-Corn-Maidens will come to congratulate you, and will pretend not to know where you were. You must not speak of that, but invite them to go out and play a game with you."

In a day or two the witch-sisters did come, with deceitful words; and the Moon invited them to go out and play a game. They went up to the edge of the llano, and there she let them get a glimpse of the pretty hoop.

"Oh, give us that, Moon-friend," they teased. But she refused. At last, however, she said:

"Well, we will play the hoop game. I will stand here, and you there; and if, when I roll it to you, you catch it before it falls upon its side, you may have it."

So the witch-sisters stood a little way down the hill, and she rolled the bright hoop. As it came trundling to them, both grasped it at the same instant; and lo! instead of the Yellow-Corn-Maidens, there were two great snakes, with tears rolling down ugly faces. The Moon came and put upon their heads a little of the pollen of the corn-blossom (still used by Pueblo snake-charmers) to tame them, and a pinch of sacred meal for their food.

"Now," she said, "you have the reward of treacherous friends. Here shall be your home among these rocks and cliffs forever, but you must never be found upon the prairie; and you must never bite a person. Remember you are women, and must be gentle."

And then the Moon went home to her husband, and they were very happy together. As for the sister snakes, they still dwell where she bade them, and never venture away; though sometimes the people bring them to their houses to catch mice, for these snakes never hurt a person.

The Laugh-maker

(SIOUX)

The village of the Bears was a large one, and the people were well-fed and prosperous. Upon certain days, a herald went the round of the lodges, announcing in a loud voice that the time had come to "go a-laughing." Not a Bear was left in the village at such times, for every one went, old and young, sick and well, the active and the lame. Only the stranger remained at home, although his wife, Woshpee, always went with her kinsfolk, for somehow he did not feel inclined to "go a-laughing;" and he kept with him his little son, who was half Bear and half human.

One day, however, a curiosity seized him to know what this laughing business might be. He took his boy and followed the Bears at a distance, not choosing to be seen. Their trail led to the shore of the Great Water, and when he had come as near as he could without exposing himself, he climbed a tall pine from whose bushy top he could observe all that took place.

The gathering of the Bears was on a deep

bay that jutted inland. Its rocky shores were quite black with them, and as soon as all had become quiet, an old Bear advanced to the water's edge and called in a loud voice:

"E-ha-we-cha-ye-la, e-ha-un-he-pee lo! (Laugh-maker, we are come to laugh!)"

When he had called four times, a small object appeared in the midst of the water and began to swim toward the shore. By and by the strange creature sprawled and clambered out upon a solitary rock that stood partly above the water.

The Laugh-maker was hairless and wrinkled like a new-born child; it had the funniest feet, or hands, or flippers, with which it tried to walk, but only tumbled and flopped about. In the water it was graceful enough, but on dry land so ungainly and ridiculous that the vast concourse of Bears was thrown into fits of hysterical laughter.

"Ha, ha, ha! Waugh, waugh!" they roared, lifting their ugly long muzzles and opening their gaping jaws. Some of them could no longer hold on to the boughs of the trees, or the rocks on which they had perched, and came tumbling down on the heads of the crowd, adding much to the fun. Every motion of the little "Laugh-maker" produced fresh roars of immoderate laughter.

At last the Bears grew weak and helpless with laughing. Hundreds of them sprawled out upon the sand, quite unable to rise. Then the old man again advanced and cried out:

"E-ha-we-cha-ye-la, wan-na e-ha un-ta-pe ktay do! (Laugh-maker, we are almost dead with laughing!)" Upon this the little creature swam back into deep water and disappeared.

Now the stranger was not at all amused and in fact could see nothing to laugh at. When all the Bears had got up and dispersed to their homes he came down from the tree with his little son, and the child wished to imitate his great-grandfather Bear. He went out alone on the sandy beach and began to call in his piping voice:

"Laugh-maker, we are come to laugh!"

When he had called four times, the little creature again showed its smooth black head above the water.

"Ha, ha, ha! Why don't you laugh, papa? It is so funny!" the boy cried out breathlessly.

But his father looked on soberly while the thing went through all its usual antics, and the little boy laughed harder and harder, until at last he rolled and rolled on the sandy beach, almost dead with laughter.

"Papa," he gasped, "if you do not stop this funny thing I shall die!"

Then the father picked up his bow and strung it. He gave one more look at his boy, who was gasping for breath; then he fitted a sharp arrow to the bow and pierced the little Laugh-maker to the heart. He went out and took the skin, and they returned in silence to the camp of the Bears.

Now the next time that the herald called upon the Bears to "go a-laughing," the skin of the Laugh-maker was almost dry, but they knew nothing of it. They went away as usual, and left the young man alone with his son. But he, knowing that his wife's kinsfolk would kill him when they discovered what he had done, took the skin for a quiver and went homeward with his child.

The Bear Man

(MICMAC)

A man went hunting in the mountains and came across a black bear, which he wounded with an arrow. The bear turned and started to run the other way, and the hunter followed, shooting one arrow after another into it without bringing it down. Now, this was a medicine bear, and could talk or read the thoughts of people without their saying a word. At last he stopped and pulled the arrows out of his side and gave them to the man, saying, "It is of no use for you to shoot at me, for you can not kill me. Come to my house and let us live together." The hunter thought to himself, "He may kill me"; but the bear read his thoughts and said, "No, I won't hurt you." The man thought again, "How can I get anything to eat?" but the bear knew his thoughts, and said, "There shall be plenty." So the hunter went with the bear.

They went on together until they came to a hole in the side of the mountain, and the bear said, "This is not where I live, but there is going to be a council here and we will see

78

what they do." They went in, and the hole widened as they went, until they came to a large cave like a townhouse. It was full of bears— old bears, young bears, and cubs, white bears, black bears, and brown bears—and a large white bear was the chief. They sat down in a corner, but soon the bears scented the hunter and began to ask, "What is it that smells bad?" The chief said, "Don't talk so; it is only a stranger come to see us. Let him alone." Food was getting scarce in the mountains, and the council was to decide what to do about it. They had sent out messengers all over, and while they were talking two bears came in and reported that they had found a country in the low grounds where there were so many chestnuts and acorns that mast was knee deep. Then they were all pleased, and got ready for a dance, and the dance leader was the one the Indians call Kalâs′-gûnăhi′ta, "Long Hams," a great black bear that is always lean. After the dance the bears noticed the hunter's bow and arrows, and one said, "This is what men use to kill us. Let us see if we can manage them, and may be we can fight man with his own weapons." So they took the bow and arrows from the hunter to try them. They fitted the arrow and drew back the string, but when they let go it caught in their long claws

They fitted the arrow and drew back the string,
but when they let go it caught in their long claws
and the arrows dropped to the ground.

and the arrows dropped to the ground. They saw that they could not use the bow and arrows and gave them back to the man. When the dance and the council were over, they began to go home, excepting the White Bear chief, who lived there, and at last the hunter and the bear went out together.

They went on until they came to another hole in the side of the mountain, when the bear said, "This is where I live," and they went in. By this time the hunter was very hungry and was wondering how he could get something to eat. The other knew his thoughts, and sitting up on his hind legs he rubbed his stomach with his forepaws—*so*—and at once he had both paws full of chestnuts and gave them to the man. He rubbed his stomach again—*so*—and had his paws full of huckleberries, and gave them to the man. He rubbed again—*so*—and gave the man both paws full of blackberries. He rubbed again—*so*—and had his paws full of acorns, but the man said that he could not eat them, and that he had enough already.

The hunter lived in the cave with the bear all winter, until long hair like that of a bear began to grow all over his body and he began to act like a bear; but he still walked like a man. One day in early spring the bear said to him, "Your people down in the settlement are getting ready for a grand hunt in these mountains, and they will come to this cave and kill me and take these clothes from me"—he meant his skin—"but they will not hurt you and will take you home with them." The bear knew what the people were doing down in the settlement just as he always knew what the man was thinking about. Some days passed and the bear said again, "This is the day when the Topknots will come to kill me, but the Split-noses will come first and find us. When they have killed me they will drag me outside the cave and take off my clothes and cut me in pieces. You must cover the blood with leaves, and when they are taking you away look back after you have gone a piece and you will see something."

Soon they heard the hunters coming up the mountain, and then the dogs found the cave and began to bark. The hunters came and looked inside and saw the bear and killed him with their arrows. Then they dragged him outside the cave and skinned the body and cut it in quarters to carry home. The dogs kept on barking until the hunters thought there must be another bear in the cave. They looked in again and saw the man away at the farther end. At first they thought it was another bear

around which they traveled for some time, and then the man took off all the boy's clothes, and, jumping into his canoe, said, "Come, swans, let us go home," and he began to sing. When the boy perceived that he was deserted he went up the bank and sat down and cried, for he was naked and cold.

It began to grow dark very fast, and he was greatly frightened when he heard a voice say, "Hist! keep still," and, looking around, he saw a skeleton on the ground near him, which beckoned him and said, "Poor boy, it was the same thing with me, but I will help you if you will do something for me." The boy readily consented. Then the skeleton told him to go to a tree near by, and dig on the west side of it, and he would find a tobacco-pouch full of tobacco, a pipe, and a flint; and the boy found them and brought them to the skeleton. It then said, "Fill the pipe and light it"; and he did so. "Put it in my mouth," said the skeleton; and he did so. Then, as the skeleton smoked, the boy saw that its body was full of mice, which went away because of the smoke. Then the skeleton felt better, and told the boy that a man with three dogs was coming to the island that night to kill him, and in order to escape he must run all over the island and jump into the water and out again many times, so that the man would lose the trail. Then, after tracking the island all over, he must get into a hollow tree near by, and stay all night. So the boy tracked the island all over and jumped into the water many times, and at last went into the tree. In the early morning he heard a canoe come ashore, and, looking out, saw another man with three dogs, to whom the man said, "My dogs, you must catch this animal." Then they ran all over the island, but not finding him, the man became so angry that he killed one of the dogs and ate him all up. Then, taking the two remaining, he went away. The boy then came out from his hiding-place, and went to the skeleton, who said, "Are you still alive?" The boy replied, "Yes." "Well," said the skeleton, "the man who brought you here will come tonight to drink your blood, and you must go down to the shore where he will come in, and dig a long pit and lie down in it and cover yourself up with the sand so he cannot see you, and when he comes ashore and is off, you must get into the canoe and say, 'Come, swans, let's go home,' and if the man calls for you to come back you must not turn around or look at him."

The boy promised to obey and soon the man who had brought him came ashore on the island. Then the boy jumped into the canoe, saying, "Come, swans, let's go to our place"; and as they went he sang just as the man had done. They had gone but a little way when the man saw them. He began to cry, "Come back! Oh, do come back!" but the boy did not look around and they kept on their way. By and by they came to a large rock in which there was a hole, and the swans went up into the rock until they came to a door which the boy proceeded to open. Upon entering the cave he found his own clothes and many others, and also a fire and food all prepared, but no living person. After putting on his clothes he went to sleep for the night. In the morning he found a fire and food, but saw no one.

Upon leaving the cave he found the swans still waiting at the entrance, and, jumping into the canoe, he said, "Come, swans, let's go to the island." When he arrived there he found the man had been killed and nearly eaten up. He then went to the skeleton, which said, "You are a very smart boy; now you must go and get your sister whom this man carried off many years ago. You must start tonight and go east, and by and by you will come to some very high rocks where she goes for water, and you will find her there and she will tell you what to do."

The boy started and in three days arrived at

the rocks, where he found his sister, to whom he called, "Sister, come, go home with me"; but she replied, "No, dear brother, I cannot go; a bad man keeps me here, and you must go, for he will kill you if he finds you here." But as the boy would not be persuaded to leave without her she allowed him to stay. Now this very bad man had gone to a great swamp where women and children were picking cranberries. The sister then went to the house and, taking up the planks over which her bed was made, she dug a pit underneath it sufficiently large for her brother to sit in; then she went to her brother and bade him follow her, and to be sure and step in her tracks and not touch anything with his hands or his clothes. So she covered him up in the pit she had prepared for him, and made her bed up again over the place. She then cooked a little boy for the man, put it with wood and water by his bed, and then went and lay down. Soon the man and dogs returned; then immediately the dogs began barking and tearing around as if they were mad. The man said, "You surely have visitors"; she replied, "None but you." And he said, "I know better"; and he took a stick and commanded her to tell him the truth, but she denied it, saying, "Kill me if you like, but I have none." He then went to his bed and sat down to eat his supper; but he said to himself, "She has some one hidden; I will kill him in the morning." He then called her to build a fire, but she replied, "You have wood, build your own fire." Then he said, "Come, take off my moccasins"; but she replied, "I am tired, take them off yourself." Then he said to himself, "Now I know she has seen some one, for she was never so saucy."

In the morning he started off for the swamp to get some children for his dinner. A short distance from home he concealed himself to watch the girl. As soon as he was gone she called her brother and said, "Come, let us take his canoe and go quickly." So they ran and jumped into the canoe and went off, but the man saw them and ran, throwing a hook which caught the canoe, but as he was pulling it ashore the boy took a stone from the bottom of the canoe and broke the hook. Then they proceeded again very fast. Then the enraged man resorted to another expedient: Laying himself down upon the shore he began to drink the water from the lake, which caused the boat to return very fast. The man continued to drink, until he grew very big with so much water in him. The boy took another stone and threw it and hit the man so it killed him, and the water ran back into the lake. When they saw that he was dead they went back, and the boy said to the two dogs, "You bad dogs, no one will have you now; you must go into the woods and be wolves"; and they started for the woods and became wolves.

Then the boy and his sister went to the island. The boy went to the skeleton, which said, "You are a very smart boy to have recovered your sister—bring her to me." This the boy did, and the skeleton continued, "Now, gather up all the bones you see and put them in a pile; then push the largest tree you see and say, 'All dead folks arise'; and they will all arise." The boy did so, and all the dead arose, some having but one arm, some with but one leg, but all had their bows and arrows.

The boy then said to his sister, "Come, let's go home." When they arrived home they found their own uncle; he looked very old. For ten years he had cried and put ashes upon his head for his little nephew, but now he was very happy to think he had returned.

The boy then told the old man all that he had done, who said, "Let us build a long house." And they did so, and put in six fireplaces. Then the boy went back to the island for his people and brought them to the house, where they lived peacefully many years.